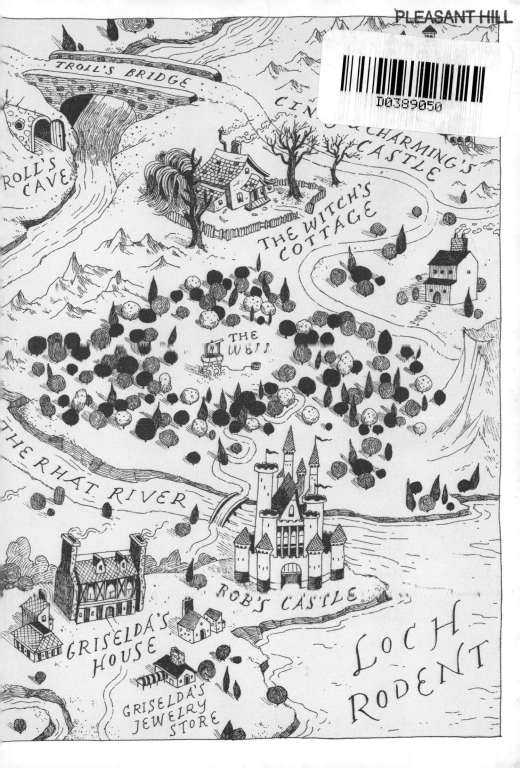

HOW TO SAVE YOUR T·A·I·L

IF YOU ARE A RAT NABBED BY CATS WHO REALLY LIKE STORIES
ABOUT MAGIC SPOONS, WOLVES WITH SNOUT–WARTS,
BIG, HAIRY CHIMNEY TROLLS . . . AND COOKIES TOO

HOW TO SAVE YOUR
T·A·I·L

**IF YOU ARE A RAT NABBED BY CATS WHO REALLY LIKE STORIES
ABOUT MAGIC SPOONS, WOLVES WITH SNOUT-WARTS,
BIG, HAIRY CHIMNEY TROLLS . . . AND COOKIES TOO**

MARY HANSON

Illustrations by John Hendrix

schwartz & wade books · new york

Published in the United States by Schwartz & Wade Books, an imprint of
Random House Children's Books, a division of Random House, Inc., New York.

Schwartz & Wade Books and colophon are trademarks of Random House, Inc.

www.randomhouse.com/kids

Educators and librarians, for a variety of teaching tools,
visit us at www.randomhouse.com/teachers

Library of Congress Cataloging-in-Publication Data

Hanson, Mary Elizabeth.
How to save your tail: if you are a rat nabbed by cats who really like stories
about magic spoons, wolves with snout-warts, big, hairy chimney trolls . . . and
cookies too/Mary Hanson; illustrated by John Hendrix.—1st ed.
p.   cm.
Summary: When he is captured by two of the queen's cats, Bob the rat
prolongs his life by sharing fresh-baked cookies and stories of his ancestors,
whose escapades are remarkably similar to those of well-known fairy tale heroes.
ISBN 978-0-375-83755-5 (trade)—ISBN 978-0-375-93755-2 (Gibraltar lib.bdg.)
[1. Storytelling—Fiction.   2. Rats—Fiction.   3. Cats—Fiction.   4. Characters in
literature—Fiction.   5. Fairy tales.]   I. Hendrix, John, ill.   II. Title.

PZ8.H1968How 2007
[Fic]

2006003833

The text of this book is set in Bembo Book.
The illustrations are rendered in pen and ink.
Book design by Rachael Cole

Printed in the United States of America

10   9   8   7   6   5   4   3   2

First Edition

For Bob and Stephanie
—M.H.

To Andrea and Jack
—J.H.

Contents

SHERMAN AND PUDDING'S
OTHER CHILDREN
Worked in trade
(cheesemongers, ditchdiggers)

CHEDDAR

NOODLE

MOZZARELLA AND BASIL'S OTHER CHILDREN
Some died of heartbreak.
Others led lives of crime.
One became a lawyer.

MUSH

DILLWEED

SONNY

CECIL

CLINKENBE

LITTLE NE

BOB'S GREAT-GRANDFATHER

BASIL

BOB'S GREAT-GREAT-GRANDFATHER
A common kitchen rat

SHERMAN

ELVIS

FROSTY

SHORTY

MOZZARELLA

GALEN

BOB'S GREAT-GRANDMOTHER
A wool spinner's helper
Later a circus tightrope artist

RUSSELL SP

PUDDING

SQUEAK

DUSTY

LEO

BOB'S GREAT-GREAT-GRANDMOTHER
A common kitchen rat
(met under the sink)

MUSTARD

BUBBLES

BOB'S GREAT-GRANDUNCLE AND -AUNTS
Builders

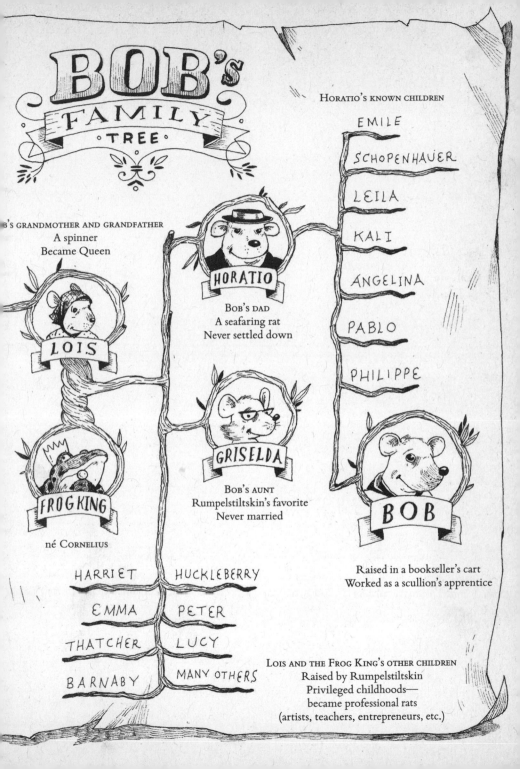

BOB's FAMILY TREE

HORATIO'S KNOWN CHILDREN

EMILE

SCHOPENHAUER

LEILA

KALI

ANGELINA

PABLO

PHILIPPE

BOB'S GRANDMOTHER AND GRANDFATHER
A spinner
Became Queen

LOIS

HORATIO

BOB'S DAD
A seafaring rat
Never settled down

FROG KING

né CORNELIUS

GRISELDA

BOB'S AUNT
Rumpelstiltskin's favorite
Never married

BOB

Raised in a bookseller's cart
Worked as a scullion's apprentice

HARRIET   HUCKLEBERRY

EMMA   PETER

THATCHER   LUCY

BARNABY   MANY OTHERS

LOIS AND THE FROG KING'S OTHER CHILDREN
Raised by Rumpelstiltskin
Privileged childhoods—
became professional rats
(artists, teachers, entrepreneurs, etc.)

Once Upon a Time

Once upon a time, in a grand castle, there lived a rat named Bob, who was fond of baking and wild about reading.

Now, baking can be dangerous for a rat. Paws get burned and tails get caught in eggbeaters all the time.

But it was his love of books that almost killed

Bob. The trouble tiptoed up on him one afternoon, while his cookies were browning in the oven. As Bob sunned himself on the kitchen porch, he watched a bee flit about the garden, from rose to rose and lily to lily, landing at last

on the garden bench—right next to
a book.

The rat sat up, tail twitching and whiskers whisking. Was it a new book? Or was it one of his favorites that he had read a hundred times? Either way, Bob was happier than a pig in a puddle. He had to have it.

Quick as a wink, he leapt from the porch to the path. He was so anxious to devour the words that he never saw the Queen's cats in the rosebushes, waiting to devour him.

VOOOMP! Something had grabbed him—something with sharp claws and bad breath. Bob smelled a cat. It was all over but the chewing.

He opened one eye and saw the orange stripes and treacherous teeth of . . . Brutus.

Then Muffin pounced into view. She

was huge, fluffy, and white as bones, except for her chin, which was stained with the blood of her last meal—a mouse, perhaps. Or a small bear.

"Head or tail?" asked Brutus.

"Head," said Muffin. "I had the tail last time."

"Okay. Grab on. When I count three, *pull!*"

Muffin grabbed. Bob squirmed. Brutus, just before counting, sniffed.

"Hey!" he said. "What's that smell?"

"Coofies?" guessed Muffin, talking with her mouth full.

"Butter cookies," said the rat. He tried to sound as casual as possible, in spite of his delicate position.

"Where?" asked Brutus.

"In the oven," squeaked the rat. "I'm

testing a new recipe: double butter with cream
cheese filling and a sinful blend of spice, mint
chips, and sugar."

The cats drooled.

"I'd hate for them to burn," added Bob.

"Me too," said Muffin, dropping the rat with
a thunk.

"Okay, Mack," said Brutus, letting go of
Bob's tail. "Get them out. But don't try anything
funny."

"Yes, sir," said Bob. "But—but—"

"But *what*?"

"My name's not Mack, sir."

"It is now," said Brutus. *"Go!"*

So Bob—*Mack* to the cats—wobbled to his
feet, shook off the cat slobber, and scurried into
the kitchen. The cats tailed him.

The kitchen was hot. The cats were hungry.
And Bob—aka Mack—was quick.

He poured two saucers of milk and served the
cookies, warm from the oven, on the Queen's
finest china.

He held his breath as the cats tasted.

"Yum," said Muffin.

"Not bad," said Brutus.

"Do you really think so?" asked Bob. "My

great-great-grandfather's were better—before he lost his spoon."

"His spoon?" asked Brutus.

"His magic spoon," said Bob. "But that's another story."

"Do tell, Mack!" said Muffin.

"No way," said Brutus. "It's time for the main course." He snatched the rat up by the scruff of his neck and dipped him in milk.

"Not yet, Brutus!" cried Muffin. "I want to hear the story!"

Brutus looked at Muffin. "Well, okay," he said. "But after the story we eat him."

Brutus dropped Bob, without ceremony, on an empty plate.

Then Bob, with great ceremony, brushed himself off, assumed his best storytelling posture, and began to tell about the day his great-great-grandfather Sherman climbed the beanstalk.

Sherman and the Beanstalk

In the days when a fellow needed a quick mind, a strong will, and a keen sense of adventure just to survive, there lived an extraordinary rat—my great-great-grandpa Sherman Rattus Norvegicus. Sherman (for short) had all those qualities plus a sharp nose and fast feet. And he did pretty well, thank you. Why, in just one week, he escaped an evil Queen who tested bad apples on good rats; dodged three bears chasing a small blond girl; and sidestepped twelve dancing Princesses who nearly trampled him to death practicing the bunny hop. Finally, he found safety in a run-down cottage with a widow and her son, Jack.

Jack was harmless enough, but let's face it—he did *not* possess a quick mind, a strong will, or any sense of adventure whatsoever. In fact, Jack never thought to wake up, get dressed, or eat breakfast until his mother suggested it.

Once, while lurking below the cottage floor, Sherman heard the widow talking to her son.

"Now, listen, Jack. The cupboards are bare and we're out of grocery money. Our clothes have holes and we're out of mending thread. We have a rat—I think—and we're out of poison. There is only one thing to do."

"Eat the rat?"

Sherman shivered.

"No, you numbnoggin," scolded the widow. "You must take the cow to market and sell her. Oh, and on the way, stop at your auntie Lou's house and give her this bread. She's feeling poorly."

"But I thought we were out of food," said Jack.

"Don't worry," said the widow. "It's moldy."

Moldy bread? Sherman's ears pricked up. Green, fuzzy, moldy bread was his absolute favorite—except for cookies.

Sherman scrabbled up through a hole in the floor and into the bread basket. Jack did not notice, and neither did his mother. They were both busy fussing with Jack's little red cape.

"Now, remember, Jack, stay on the path and

never wander off it even an inch—for that way
lie bad, scary, awful, terrible, nasty things."

Jack promised to obey. He took up the basket,
tied a rope to the cow, and started on his way.

Sherman bounced along in the basket,
nibbling at the moldy loaf, and thanked his lucky
fleas for the chance of adventure, which he loved
more than anything—except cookies.

They had not gone far when Jack, steadfast on
the path, bumped into something. He fell down,
dropped his basket, and lost his cow.

Sherman tumbled out into the grass, looked
up, and blinked. Above him towered an
enormous, stupendous, humongous, very tall
beanstalk. His nose quivered. Coming from
somewhere, Sherman was not sure where, was the
smell of . . . cookies. Fresh, warm, just-out-of-
the-oven cookies. *Hot chocolaty-chips!* thought
Sherman.

"Gosh," said Jack, for he too noticed the beanstalk. Then he gathered up the bread and basket and started back on his path, looking for his cow.

Sherman was stunned.

"Jack!" he cried. *"How can you . . . ? Why don't we . . . ? Don't you want to . . . ?"*

But Jack trudged on, calling his cow.

Sherman, on the other paw, jumped onto the closest beanstalk leaf and started climbing. In the first place, as you will remember, there was nothing he loved more than adventure—except cookies, of course. In the second place, as you have probably guessed, he was now 100 percent sure the cookie smell was coming from the top of the beanstalk.

It was a long climb, but there were yummy bean blossoms along the way, not to mention a spectacular view. At last, he reached the tip-top of the beanstalk, stepped onto an oh-so-cushy cloud, and saw an immense castle. The smell of cookies was everywhere.

An oven timer pinged.

Sherman made a beeline for the castle and climbed in through a window. He pointed his nose in the direction of the cookie smell and dashed toward it, down a long, shiny hall, past the parlor, and into the kitchen.

There they were, in giant jars, on ponderous plates, and cooling on colossal cookie racks— hundreds and hundreds of monstrous, magnificent, mouthwatering cookies. Sherman looked everywhere, beneath chairs, atop counters, inside cupboards, and behind the door. He saw no one. Not a single soul. So he dove into the nearest platter to fill his belly with chocolate chips and crispy crumbs.

He was still stuffing his cheeks when the cook came in with a wild look on her round, red face.

"There you are!" she bellowed.

The jig is up, thought Sherman. *I'm rat-meat.* He squeezed behind the breadbox.

But the cook wasn't talking to Sherman. She reached, instead, for a spoon.

"Spoon!" she said, placing it in a bowl,

"Stir and swirl
Sugar and butter,
Beat and blend

Eggs and spice.
Chocolate chips?
Measure them twice.
Cookies for Master,
Faster and faster!"

Then, in a blink of an eye and a twitch of a
tail, the spoon measured, mixed, and baked a
batch of giant cookies out of *nothing at all*.

Sherman went dizzy with wonder.

The smell of a new batch brought something
dreadful to the kitchen—something no rat
should ever see, not even in his worst nightmare.
The thing stood on its hulking hind legs in the
middle of the room. It was covered with coarse
black fur, and a jagged scar marked its cheek
from one ragged ear to its grizzled snout-
whiskers. A bad overbite revealed sharp,
greenish, unbrushed fangs, and it was as big

as a whale. It was a giant, yes. But worse, it was a cat . . . in boots.

The frightful feline scooped up a pawful of cookies with his claws, shoved them into his mouth, and sniffed the air.

> *"Fee, fi, fo, fum—*
> *I smell a rat."*

Before Sherman could wiggle a whisker, the overgrown cat reached behind the breadbox and snatched him by the tail.

"He'll make a tasty tidbit, don't you think, Cook?"

"Ah, yes. We'll skin him, roast him, and set him atop your parsnips with a sprig of parsley."

The giant drooled and dropped Sherman into the cook's hands. Then he grabbed another dozen cookies and stomped out of the kitchen.

The cook opened the pantry door and plunked Sherman into a roomful of darkness. The door slammed, and the rat was alone.

Or so he thought.

"G-g-greetings."

"Who's there?" asked Sherman.

"Just me, Justine."

"Well, Justine," said Sherman, "nice to meet you. Name's Sherman. Is he going to eat you too?"

"I th-th-think so," sniffled Justine. Then she grunted. "Oh dear. Not an-n-n-nother one!"

Suddenly, something shone in the darkness. Something golden.

Sherman blinked. It looked like an egg. He scrabbled over to it.

"Wow!"

"P-please don't tell anyone," begged Justine.

Sherman looked at her in the glow of the egg. Justine was a goose.

"Why not?" he asked.

"It's not a p-p-proper egg, is it?"

"But it's made of gold!" said Sherman.

"Solid gold!" wailed Justine. "Nothing ever hatches! And they're heavy. I can't do a thing with them."

"Them?"

Justine waddled over to a heap of empty flour sacks. She took a corner of one in her bill and waddled backward. The sack slid off something glimmery. She continued to pull sack after sack away, uncovering a huge pile of golden eggs. Then she wagged her head and gaggled forth a flood of tears.

"I'm so emb-b-barrassed!"

"Don't worry," soothed Sherman. "I won't tell a soul."

Too late. The door creaked open and the cook came in with her axe.

Sherman and Justine froze.

So did the cook—dropping the axe on her own toe. And though her toe was chopped off and her best shoes were ruined, she stood stone still, dazzled silly by the golden eggs.

"*Go!*" said Sherman, and they did. With skittering feet and flapping wings, the rat and the goose gave the cook the slip.

But just at the kitchen door, Sherman remembered something.

"*Stop!*" he shouted, and they did. Then Sherman climbed the table leg and came back down with the spoon in his mouth. It was three times bigger than Sherman, but a rat can do amazing things for the right reason.

Off they raced again—out of the kitchen, past the parlor, and down the hall.

BAM! BAM! BAM! The cat giant pounded out of the parlor door. He snorted and roared and hissed and before you could say "Fee fi," he was at Sherman's heels.

"Lay an egg!" said Sherman, through clenched teeth and magic spoon, and Justine did.

The egg dropped to the ground, rolled under the giant's massive boots, and sent him crashing to the floor.

Justine flew low, and Sherman jumped on her back. They flapped out the window and made a gooseline for the beanstalk. Sherman showed Justine the way down. They could just begin to see the path below when they heard the giant smash through the castle door.

Sherman dropped the spoon and cried, *"Jump!"* And they did.

With the rat hanging tight to Justine's neck, they flapped and plummeted and landed on a haystack.

When Sherman looked up, he could see the mammoth cat climbing down through the clouds.

Sherman thought fast. Then he chewed— right through the beanstalk.

BOOM! The giant fell to the earth, dead as dirt.

At that moment, Jack trudged out of the woods, head down, eyes on the path.

"Why so sad?" asked Sherman.

"Lost my cow," said Jack.

"Here," said Sherman. "Have a goose." He winked at Justine and whispered, "Don't worry. Jack won't mind about the eggs."

Then Sherman scurried off to find his magic spoon.

And the cow.

After all, what good are cookies without milk?

Cookie Break

"Did that goose really lay golden eggs?" asked Muffin.

"Sure," said Bob. "And her sister, Stephanie, laid colored eggs that actually hatched. Her goslings came in all the colors of the rainbow. In fact, one of her daughters, Blue Sue, lives down by the Royal Pond. She's a good friend of mine."

"Who cares? Story over," said Brutus.

"Did Sherman find the spoon?" asked Muffin.

"Too many questions," said Brutus. "Time to eat the rat."

Bob squiggled backward off the plate. He bumped into Brutus's waiting claws and squiggled back on.

"I want to know!" insisted Muffin.

Brutus pouted and looked at Bob. "Well?"

"He—he did find the spoon," said Bob. "And—and the cow."

"Then what happened, Mack?" asked Muffin. "Did he get fat and juicy and taste like chocolate chips?"

"Well, Grandpa Sherman was a t-tad portly, but I don't know about the juicy part," said Bob, a bit weak in the knees. "That's beside the point. What happened next is that he went back to the beanstalk stump and found that the big

puss had turned to dust and blown away, leaving
nothing but his boots—which Sherman moved
into. Now, if I'd been in those boots, I would
have put comfy chairs in the toes and spent
my days reading and baking cookies. But
nooooooo. Sherman got married! Then he had
so many children he didn't know what to do.
And one day, at his youngest daughter's birthday
party, some of her naughty friends chewed up
the spoon."

"*Oh no!*" cried Muffin.

"Oh yes," said Bob. "After that, there was
nothing to eat and all the children had to make
their own way in the world—but that's another
story."

"Tell us!" said Muffin.

Bob washed a paw and swallowed a little
smile.

"Hey!" Brutus glowered at Muffin.

"Don't you
want to hear about Sherman's
children?" asked Muffin.

"Only if he tells us where
they live," said Brutus with a
flash of his fangs, "so we can
eat them after we eat him."

"Sounds good," said Muffin.
She looked at Bob. "Let's hear it, Mack."

"Well," said the rat, "there were so many kids.
Which one do you want to hear about?"

"The biggest, fattest, juiciest one," said Brutus, licking his chops.

"That would be my great-granduncle Mustard. He took care of his little sisters, Bubbles and Squeak, who were both on the small side."

"You don't say," said Muffin.

"I do say," said the rat. "And poor Squeak had a gimpy leg."

"Just get on with it!" growled Brutus.

"Okay, okay," said Bob, and he began at the beginning, with the problems the three rats had finding a nice place to live.

The Three Rats

Once, in a rough neighborhood, my great-granduncle Mustard and my two great-grandaunties, Bubbles and Squeak, tried living in a house of straw. When a certain someone puffed and huffed it down, they tried living in a house of sticks. And when the same someone blew the sticks to smithereens, they built themselves a lovely three-bedroom, two-bath brick house with a cellar.

No sooner did they build it than the very same neighbor, the Big Bad Wolf, to be exact, took a liking to the fancy brickwork and homey front stoop. And one fine day he showed up with his family.

"This is Mrs. Wolf and our daughter, Elsie," said Big Bad. "We're moving in."

Elsie had foul breath and warts on her snout.

"You're *not* moving in!" said Mustard.

"Not by the hair on our chinny-chin-chins," said Bubbles.

"We don't have chins," whispered Mustard.

"Oh dear," said Squeak.

"Unpack our bags," ordered Elsie. "Then make dinner." A drip of slobber slid down her lip and off her chin.

The rats gulped.

"And don't even think about running away," said Big Bad. "Or *you'll* be dinner."

"Yeah," said Elsie. "I love rat salad and rat sandwiches and most of all I love rat pudding for dessert." She stomped on Squeak's tail just for fun.

So, from that day forward, Mustard, Bubbles, and Squeak worked for the wolves and lived in the cellar. Every morning, Elsie pinched their ears to wake them. If the rats were too slow scrubbing the floor or weeding the garden or ironing her clothes, she made them pluck and roast their bird friends for supper. Squeak never did get over the heartbreak of cooking her best friend, Robin. Then, at night, after they washed the dishes, Elsie made them tell bedtime stories while she gnawed on bird bones and picked at her snout-warts.

She was a lousy roommate.

"I can't take it anymore!" cried Squeak one

morning after Elsie pinched their ears, their tails, *and* their toes.

"We have to get rid of her," agreed Mustard.

"How?" asked Bubbles.

"I've got it," said Mustard. "We'll tell everyone that Elsie is the cleverest maiden in the land. Surely someone will marry her and they'll both move far, far away and we'll never get pinched again."

So the rats went about the town, hiding behind fences, under tables, and in laundry baskets. They talked about Clever Elsie Wolf in their biggest voices, and the nosy townsfolk were only too happy to eavesdrop and pass along the gossip. Sure enough, before you could say "Hot cross buns," word of Clever Elsie spread far and wide throughout the kingdom.

By and by, a rich and powerful warthog paid a visit to discuss marriage. Elsie's parents wanted to

celebrate the wedding at once, but the warthog had a few questions.

"What makes Elsie so clever?" he asked.

Elsie's parents looked at each other, baffled. For though they had heard the rumor of Elsie's newfound cleverness and though they hoped it was true, they had not yet seen a shred of evidence that it was. They thought and thought but could not come up with a single instance of Elsie's doing anything that wasn't disgusting or mean or just plain dull.

The three rats spoke up.

"Well," said Mustard, "she can see the wind before the storm."

"And she knew not to trust that little girl in the red hood," added Bubbles and Squeak.

"Are you saying," queried the warthog, "that she can see the future?"

"That's *it*!" said Mustard.

"Just so! Just so!" cried Bubbles and Squeak.

"Ahhh," said the warthog. "Well, I didn't get rich and powerful by believing any old thing. I'll need proof." He turned to Elsie. "What do you see now, Miss Wolf?"

Elsie squinted hard but spoke not a word.

"Sometimes it takes a while," said Mustard. "Have a seat."

The warthog sat down and Big Bad sent Elsie to the cellar for cider.

The rats followed.

"We must do something," whispered Mustard.

"But what?" asked Bubbles and Squeak.

"I'm thinking," said Mustard.

Elsie ordered the rats to fill the pitcher and stepped on poor Squeak's bad foot for good measure. Mustard scrambled up the side of a great wooden keg and opened the spout.

"You know, Elsie," said Mustard as cider

poured into the pitcher, "if you marry the warthog, you might have a son."

"Yes," said Bubbles. "He would be a fearsome creature indeed."

"Fangs, warts, *and* tusks!" squeaked Squeak.

"That would be marvelous!" said Elsie.

"But," said Mustard, "what if . . . Oh, I cannot bear to think it!"

"What if *what*?" asked Elsie.

"No, no, I cannot say it!"

"You must!" cried Elsie.

"Yes, yes! You must!" said Bubbles and Squeak.

"Well, okay," said Mustard. "What if your son fetches cider one day for you and the warthog?"

"He's a dear boy," said Elsie.

"Yes, of course," said Mustard. "But perhaps, while he's down here, that shelf up there, which *may* have termites, falls down and . . . well . . . you know."

Elsie and Bubbles and Squeak all looked up. There on the shelf, smack-dab above them, were three big barrels, filled with apple cider. "Oh my," said Elsie.

"Oh dear oh dear oh dear!" added Bubbles and Squeak.

"Yes," said Mustard, "it would be terrible. Smashed warthog-wolf." He began to sniff.

Bubbles whimpered.

Squeak moaned.

Elsie howled.

Upstairs, the wolves and the warthog got antsy. After a while Big Bad spoke up.

"Wife," he said, "go down to the cellar and see what clever thing Elsie is doing."

Mrs. Wolf went down and found Elsie and the

rats weeping by the cider keg. "What's wrong, dear?" she asked.

"I might marry the warthog," said Elsie, "and have a fearsome son, and one day, the cider barrels will crush him to mush." Then she sniveled herself into another fit of slobbery sobs.

"You *can* foresee the future! Then you truly *must* be clever!" exclaimed Mrs. Wolf, delighted that Elsie had *any* talent at all. "But oh! My poor fearsome grandson—I cannot bear to lose him in such a wretched way!" And the mother wailed and lamented the tragedy along with her daughter.

Upstairs, the warthog waxed impatient.

"I'll go myself," said Big Bad, "and see what keeps them."

In the cellar, he found Mrs. Wolf and Elsie ankle deep in tears.

The three rats huddled together on a dry box in the corner.

When Big Bad asked what the problem was and Elsie started to explain, the rats saw their chance. They made a break for it.

Mustard, Bubbles, and Squeak were halfway across the cellar when Big Bad spotted them.

"Oh no you don't!" he hollered.

Elsie grabbed a shovel with the clever idea of bonking their little heads. Instead, she hit the

shelf, which really did have termites. It crumbled and the barrels crashed down and rolled over one, two, three wolves, leaving them flat as pattycakes.

"Oh well," said the warthog, who saw the whole thing from the cellar door. "That's that." He grabbed his hat and set off to look for another clever maiden.

The three rats climbed the stairs, closed the cellar door behind them, and sealed it up with a new brick wall.

After that, they moved back into their own bedrooms, made a small fortune as bricklayers specializing in fancy chimneys, and lived happily ever after.

Cookie Break

"Yuck," groaned Muffin. "How do you get snout-warts, Mack?"

"By being mean and evil," said Bob, looking Brutus right in the eye.

"Elsie should have eaten those rats while she had the chance," said Brutus. "Like when they were telling stories."

Bob skittered under a lacy linen napkin and
shivered.

"Did the rats ever see the warthog again?"
asked Muffin.

"Yes," said Bob, peeking out from beneath the
napkin. "They built his chimney."

"Did the warthog ever get married?"

"As a matter of fact, he married the three rats'
niece—my grandma Lois—but that's another
story."

"Wow!" said Muffin. "I want to hear all
about it!"

"I don't think so," said Brutus,
preparing to pounce. "We had a deal,
remember, Muffin? Stories first—we did that
part—and now . . . a crunchy, chewy bedtime
snack."

The rat piped up from under the napkin. "You
did have a deal," he said. "But you know, this

particular story is *about* a deal. Too bad you won't get to hear it."

"Please, Brutus?" purred Muffin. "Pretty please with tuna on top?"

Brutus melted. "This better be good, Mack," he said. His stomach growled. "Are there any more cookies?"

So the rat gave each cat another cookie and some fresh milk and told them about Mustard, Squeak, and Bubbles's niece, Lois, who knew what it meant to be hungry, how to work hard (sort of), and the joys of raising a family.

The Chimney Troll

Once upon a time, after her mother ran away with the circus, my stunning but starving grandma Lois wandered the countryside looking for a job. By and by, she came to a castle with a sign on the door:

Now, Lois did not know whether she could spin a roomful of straw into gold, but she figured it was worth a try.

She knocked on the castle door, introduced herself to the housekeeper, and followed her to a big room stuffed with straw. A spinning wheel topped by a golden spindle stood near the fireplace.

"You must spin all of this into gold by tomorrow's dawn," said the housekeeper, "or die a grisly death."

"Land sakes," worried Lois, once she was alone. "The sign didn't say anything about death. And, and . . . this room is soooooo big!" She tried the door, but it was locked. She looked for a

window, but the straw reached all the way to the ceiling. She thought about tunneling through the straw to find a mousehole, but she just didn't have the strength. At last, she decided there was nothing for it but to begin spinning.

Lois trod the wheel and drew a thread that was fine, smooth, and handsome. But it was not gold. Worse yet, by midnight she had spun only one small skein.

"Oh, my pink nose and yellow teeth!" she cried. "I shall never spin the straw to gold by dawn and shall die a grisly death!" At this thought, she wept so bitterly that she didn't notice the ugly little man who tumbled out of the fireplace.

"*Hey!*" he shouted. "What's with the racket?"

Lois squealed in surprise. "Who are you?" she asked, horrified by his dirty hair, long arms, and unruly tail.

"I'm the Castle Chimney Troll," he said.
"They call me Rumpelstiltskin. What's the
problem?" His red eyes squinted as if blinded by
her stunning good looks.

Lois could not know he was just plain
nearsighted.

"I said I could spin straw to gold so that I
could become Queen, but I can't spin it to gold
at all, and if it's not done by dawn I'm dead,"
she said.

"Not to worry, goodness no," said the Troll.
"I will spin the gold. But in return, you must
promise that, after you marry the King, you will
give me your firstborn child."

Lois had a good heart and did not want to give
away her firstborn, but she realized that there
would not be a firstborn if she was dead. So,
being a practical creature, she said "Okay."

The Troll set to work at once and the whirr of

the spinning wheel hummed Lois to sleep. When she woke, the first sunbeams sparkled through the window on piles and piles of spun gold. A note on the golden spindle read:

"Remember your promise. Signed, Troll."

The housekeeper arrived a moment later. She clapped and chortled and pinched Lois's whiskery cheek, which was rosy with relief. "It's so lovely," exclaimed the housekeeper, "not to have to plan another grisly death!" Then off she bustled to plan the wedding.

The King turned out to be a warthog, but when they kissed at the ceremony he changed into a frog. *Oh well,* thought Lois, *nobody's perfect*.

In time, Lois gave birth, and joy filled the household. But that night, at the grand celebration, the Chimney Troll popped into the ballroom.

"It's time to complete our bargain, Your Majesty," he said. "You owe me your firstborn."

Lois sobbed. The servants were distraught beyond words, and the Frog King was hopping mad.

But the Troll said, "A deal is a deal."

And so, in the end, Lois, as true to her word as ever a rat was, gave him her firstborn.

The Troll was so delighted with his prize—and so nearsighted—that he still did not notice that Lois was a rat and that her firstborn was a litter of thirteen baby rats. He took the basket and headed for the chimney.

"But Mr. Troll," said Lois, "a chimney is no place to raise a family."

"Don't be silly," said the Troll. "I've got a country place under the bridge by Billy Goat Hill. We'll be most comfortable there." And *zip!*

He was up the chimney and out into the wide world.

It was not until the Troll got home, warmed a bottle of milk, and lifted the blanket that he realized he had more babies than he had bargained for.

The babies woke up, and since they had a little

of their frog-dad in them, began croaking. And since the Troll had only two hands and the babies were always hungry, the croaking went on day and night. And since baby frog-rats are wiggly *and* hoppy, every time he tried to change one little diaper, the others wiggled or hopped away and the Troll was forever chasing them this way and that, under bridge and over hill.

In no time, the babies grew and each asserted its own individual personality. One slurped his food. Another never flushed the toilet. Another left half-eaten sardines under the Troll's bed. One put half-eaten chicken pot pie inside his pillowcase. One stuck chewing gum in the Troll's hair while he napped. One threw up in his slippers. One blew bubbles in pea soup. Another thought this so funny, she laughed till she snorted the soup out her snout. One repeated everything the Troll said. One burped with her mouth open. Another chewed bugs with her mouth open. One even tied up the Troll with twine while another pulled out his long, gray whiskers, one at a time.

They all jumped on the beds and left muddy pawprints everywhere and played rock-and-roll music and chewed the Troll's shoes and scurried around on the bridge late at night going "Trip trap, trip trap" and crawled into his underpants—while he was wearing them.

Finally, there came a day when the Troll decided he'd had one too many whiskers ripped from his face. He stuffed the rats in a sack and took them back to the castle.

The Troll knocked on the door, and the housekeeper showed him in. She took him to the throne room.

"I've brought your children back, Your Majesty," the Troll said.

"How thoughtful," said Lois, "but no, thanks. We have enough already." Just then, eighty-two baby frog-rats tumbled through the throne room, playing leapfrog with muddy paws. "After all," she reminded him, "a deal is a deal."

And so the Troll had no choice but to throw the sack of babies over his hunched back, turn on his hairy heel, and shuffle out of the castle with his tail between his legs.

He was so frazzled, he began talking to himself on the way home.

"Geeze, Rumple. You had a great life— wallowing in ashes, rummaging through garbage, picking on billy goats. Remember that? But you had to go and ruin it, didn't you? 'Let's adopt!' you said. Now look. Never a moment of peace. Rats croaking you up at the crack of dawn. Rats making you play hide-and-seek all the time, and you're always *It*. Rats begging for a pet snail and you end up having to feed it. I don't care if it *is* a cute snail. What were you thinking?"

Just then, Griselda, the smallest rat of all, chewed a hole through the sack, crawled up onto the Troll's shoulder, and hummed a little song.

As she nuzzled next to his neck, the baby's whiskers tickled the Troll's big, hairy ear and melted his old Troll heart.

"Maybe it's not so bad after all," he said, and decided then and there to make the best of things.

And in time, the Troll learned to like rock and roll, shaved his whiskers, bought bigger underpants, and, along with his little family, lived happily ever after.

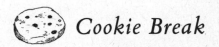 *Cookie Break*

"**P**lease tell me that Rumple-what's-his-name eventually got wise and ate the little boogers," said Brutus.

"Of course not," said Bob. "One never eats one's own family."

"I'm glad the Troll and the babies lived happily ever after," said Muffin.

"Well, actually, I exaggerated. It wasn't *ever* after," said the rat. "Only for a time. One day, the Troll married a dreadful shrew who nagged him to death. After that, all the children took off to make their fortunes—except my aunt Griselda and her ugly stepsister."

"Why did your aunt stay?"

"Just too mousy, I guess," said Bob.

"Did she stay forever?" asked Muffin.

"No," said Bob. "You see, there was this fairy—but that's another story."

"Oh, we *have* to hear this one," said Muffin. "I love fairies!"

"Another time, another place," said Brutus. "Like in a half hour or so, from inside my stomach." He squirted mustard on the rat's head. "Come on, Mack, time to go . . . and I mean *go*! Pass the ketchup, Muffin."

Bob shook the mustard off his head. No point in looking *too* delicious.

"Oh, Brutus . . ."

"Don't even start, Muffin," said Brutus. "The only subject I'm interested in is eating small, pointy-nosed mammals."

"Well, you know, sir," offered the rat, "that actually happens in this tale."

"What?" asked Brutus.

"Small, pointy-nosed mammals," said Bob. "Eaten with relish. Devoured for dinner. Enjoyed a great deal, I imagine."

"See?" said Muffin. "It'll be great . . . and
tasty . . . and icky . . . and . . ."

"Oh, all right," said Brutus. "But this is the
last, and I mean *last* story."

So Bob wiped a mustard smudge from his
nose, and the cats settled down to hear all about
Griselda and the fairy she met in the woods.

The Wood Fairy

Anyone who knows her will tell you that my aunt Griselda has always had a heart of gold, snow white fur, and the brightest, beadiest eyes anywhere. They'll also tell you that it was a wretched twist of fate when hard times forced her to share a cottage with two shrews.

The shrews happened to be her evil

stepmother and stepsister. They poked Griselda
with their sharp claws and made her do all
the work.

One day, the shrewmother sent my aunt into
the woods to gather berries.

"And mind," said the shrewsister, twisting
Griselda's tail, "that they are plump and juicy."

It was early winter, and Griselda had to search
a long time to find any berries at all—plump or
not. When at last her basket was full, the poor
thing was pinched with hunger. She feared her
shrewmother would feed her to a fox if she ate
any berries, so she pushed on until she came
to a well, where she could at least have a sip
of water.

As she drew water from the well, a scraggly
old mouse crept into view.

"Madam Whiskers," said Griselda. "You are
looking poorly. May I help you to a drink?"

The old mouse hobbled closer. She was frightfully pale.

"Or perhaps a berry will put the roses back in your cheeks." Griselda held out the basket. *Surely the shrews will not miss just one small berry,* she thought.

But the mouse, who was really a wood fairy, drank every drop of water and gobbled *every* berry. When she was refreshed, she spoke to the little rat.

"You are a dear soul," said the Fairy. "And now, in return for your kindness, I have a gift:

> *"Diamonds and pearls*
> *Each word you speak,*
> *Shimmering gems*
> *For the tiniest squeak."*

"Thank you, ma'am, but you needn't—" said Griselda, and as she spoke, three diamonds, two pearls, and one ruby fell from her mouth and into her basket. "That's odd," she said, and out popped two emeralds.

When Griselda arrived home, her

shrewmother flew at
her in a fury for being
just three minutes late.
"Give me the berries!"
snarled the shrewsister, and
she grabbed the basket. The
gems tumbled to the floor.

Then, as Griselda told them
about the raggedy old mouse,
twenty-nine sapphires slipped
from her lips.

In a twitch, the shrewmother
ordered her own daughter into the
woods. "Remember to butter up that old
mouse," she said, "and I mean tail to
whisker."

"I will be as sweet as tree sap," said the
shrewsister, "and get all I deserve."

Now, fairies are notorious changelings, and

the Wood Fairy, it so happened, changed herself
that very day. When the shrewsister reached the
well, she saw nothing but a cricket.

"Pity me, miss. I am so thirsty. Will you help
me to a wee sip of water?"

"Get it yourself, bug-face," sniped the
shrewsister. And she flicked the cricket into
the well.

The Fairy, however, was an excellent flyer and
landed neatly in the
bucket.

When the
shrewsister
raised the

bucket and tipped it to drink, she came nose to nose with the wet cricket.

"Such manners must be repaid," sputtered the cricket. "And I have the perfect reward."

The shrewsister guessed at once that the cricket was, in fact, the Wood Fairy. She curtsied and whined and offered to dry the dear thing's wings.

"Silence!" said the Fairy.

The shrewsister shut her mouth, squeezed her eyes closed, and waited for her reward.

Then, drenched in well water and shivering in the chill of twilight, the Fairy intoned her magic words:

"For all the care
you share with others;

Take my gift—
to share with your mother."

Though the shrewsister had no idea what
any of this meant, she was well pleased. Without
bothering to say "Thank you," she hurried
home to find her mother pacing at the
door.

"It's about time," said
the old shrew. "What
happened?"

"Oh, don't get
your fuzz in a
bunch," snipped
the daughter.
And with
that, five
frogs and
three toads

hopped from her mouth. "Ewwwwww!" she squealed, and out slid a snake that swallowed both shrews whole.

With no one left to order her around, Griselda moved into town, opened a jewelry store, and lived happily ever after.

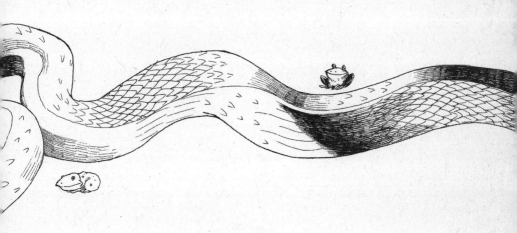

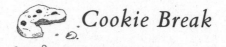Cookie Break

"Oh come on," said Brutus. "I never met a mouse who could make diamonds come out of my mouth."

"That's because the minute you meet them you eat them," said Muffin.

"Whatever," said Brutus. "Does Griselda sell cat collars with rubies?"

"Yes," said Bob, "and bracelets and earrings and tiaras. Everyone shops there. Even the Prince went to her for an engagement ring—but that's another story."

"You mean *our* Queen's son? The one who used to live in this very castle?" asked Muffin. "Prince *Charming*?"

"That kid is nuts!" said Brutus. "Remember when he used to pretend he was a horse and trotted around all day going *klop klop klop*?"

"Yes," said Muffin. "And sometimes, when he thought no one was looking, he whinnied and neighed and did horse tricks."

"I still can't figure out why that Cindy person married him," said Brutus.

"I know exactly how it happened," said the rat. "But you don't want any more stories, right?"

"You *did* say that, Brutus."

"Can it, Muffin," said Brutus. He hooked a claw around the rat's scrawny neck.

Bob's ears, tiny though they were, drooped.

"Look, Mack, I'll tell you when I've had enough stories. Got it?"

"Maybe just one more story, then," said Bob, smiling his most cooperative smile. "And I must say that the hero in this one is as brilliant and daring as he is good-looking."

"Give me a break," said Brutus. "A rat is a rat is a plain old rat."

"Don't be so sure," said Bob.

Bob's Slipper

Once upon a cottage hearth, in a warm hollow between the stones, there lived a charming, handsome, smart, and well-mannered rat named Bob. Bob loved to read. Unhappily, though, the cottage belonged to a witch, who never read anything. Her only book was *Hansel and Gretel and Other Recipes*.

Bob read the cookbook over and over again
until he was so bored he began to write his own
stories. He wrote about everyone he knew—the
butcher, the baker, the candlestick maker, and
that horrible witch.

Bob read his stories to the witch's servant girl,
Cindy. Cindy hated being cooped up in the
cottage, and she was sick of sweeping the fireplace.
She wanted to get out and kick up her heels.

Nearby, in a castle, lived a Prince named
Charming. He was crazy for horses. He spent so
much time talking to his horses that the King and
Queen were afraid he would forget how to talk to
people. For that reason, they announced a gala
party and invited every maiden in the kingdom.

Bob and Cindy were both tickled pink when
the invitation arrived at the cottage. Bob was
happy he had something new to read, even if it
was a bit short:

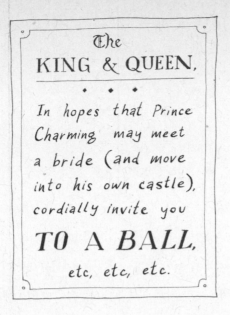

The
KING & QUEEN,

• • •

In hopes that Prince
Charming may meet
a bride (and move
into his own castle),
cordially invite you

TO A BALL,

etc, etc, etc.

Cindy was thrilled at the chance of an evening out. She danced about the kitchen with a song on her lips and Bob in her pocket. Birds fluttered to the window to sing along.

Suddenly, a spine-tingling cackle split the air. *The witch!* The birds flew off.

Cindy had forgotten about the No Singing rule.

The old hag flew into the room, and Bob peeked through a tattered hole in Cindy's pocket.

"Don't think *you're* going to the ball," snarled the witch when she saw the invitation. She ripped the card from Cindy's hand and left, as quickly as she had come.

A teardrop splashed on Bob's head. He looked up.

Cindy blew her nose.

"I wish . . . Oh, how I wish . . ."

Presto-bingo, from out of nowhere, in a puff of purple smoke, popped a little lady with wings.

She had a sparkly wand, a big book, and a
nervous twitch.

Bob climbed out of Cindy's pocket to get a
closer look.

"I—am—your—Fairy—Godmother," said
the lady, reading from her book.
"My name is—Twinkle.
Wish do you what? I mean,
what—do—
you—wish?"

Cindy blew her
nose. Again. "To go
to the ball, please," she
said. "And wear silver and
gold and dance under the
stars and meet the
Prince and eat
something new and
different and—"

"Goodness sakes alive," said Twinkle. "Please slow down. This is my first job and I'm a bit rattled."

Just then, with a screech, the witch burst into the kitchen. Twinkle poofed away in fright. Bob skooched under the rug, and the witch dragged Cindy away to sweep gingerbread crumbs.

The kitchen was quiet.

Bob skooched back out and spotted Twinkle's wand and book. He could not resist. He flipped through pages and pages of mysterious magical words. One charm reminded him of his friend Blue Sue, a niece of Justine's. I'm sure you remember Justine. She was the goose who laid the golden eggs. Anyway, it was a catchy little thing. It started: *Blue goose, true goose,* and so on and so forth. Bob smiled, but then he remembered Cindy and turned the page.

"Look!" he said when Cindy returned.

"It's a book of spells! And I found one
for you!"

"Really?" she asked.

"Sort of," he said. "It's called 'Perfect for
Parties.' It looks like it includes everything—
dress, slippers, fancy hairstyle—
everything."

"Okay," Cindy said.

The witch shrieked from the parlor. Again.

"But hurry!" said Cindy.

"Icanbeyourhorseandweneedapumpkinfora
coach," said Bob.

"I don't have a pumpkin," said Cindy. "Only a
seed."

"That will have to do," said Bob. "Now be
still."

But Cindy was too excited to be still. When
Bob waved the wand, slowly intoning, *"Sparkle
and splendor, scribbily scrat,"* Cindy turned a

cartwheel, knocked over a chair, and banged into the broom. It was very distracting. And noisy. Bob lost his place in the spell. The witch must have heard the racket, because she stormed in and grabbed the book.

It's now or never, Bob figured, and guessed the rest: *"Pumpkins and ponies—poofily splat."*

Okay, okay, so it wasn't a great guess.

Glitter swirled about the kitchen. Bob's legs felt funny. When the air cleared, his handsome fur was gone. He was smooth and silky and much too tall. Instead of a tail and whiskers, he wore glass slippers and a blue gown. A diamond tiara encircled his head and, if truth be told, Bob was the fairest maiden in the land.

Bob looked at Cindy, who was now a magnificent white horse adorned with a golden saddle and silver feathers.

The witch had turned into a pumpkin.

The pumpkin seed was still just a pumpkin seed.

"Oops," said Bob. His new voice was soft and sweet.

Cindy snorted. "Shall we go?"

"But . . . but . . ."

"But what?" asked Cindy. "I'm wearing gold and silver. I can go to the ball. And who knows, maybe I can still meet the Prince and dance under the stars."

"Okay," said Bob. "But we can't stay long. It

says here that the magic ends at midnight, and I don't wish to be under all those feet when I turn back into myself."

Trumpets blared as the fair maiden rode up to the palace on the golden horse. The maiden smiled, and the horse tossed its head and flared its nostrils.

Prince Charming was thunderstruck.

The King and Queen swooned and sighed. "Our baby's in love!"

Charming helped the maiden down from the saddle. Their eyes met.

Then off he rode on the horse.

While Cindy pranced under the stars with Charming and ate rare grasses from faraway lands, Bob was the toast of the ball. He smiled and danced and chatted with the King and Queen.

"It's a pleasure to meet you, Miss—?"

"Bob," said Bob.

"Yes, Miss Bob. Miss Bob, say hello to the Duke."

Miss Bob dazzled palace partygoers. Then he—I mean she—well, you know who I mean— heaped a plate with cheese puffs, pork rinds, and apple pie, and stole off to the library to read.

Hours ticked by.

At length, Miss Bob heard Cindy neigh beneath the window. *One minute to midnight!* The maiden dashed through the castle, out the door, and into the moonlight. Below him, Cindy waited at the foot of the stairs, Charming still on her back.

Miss Bob hurried down the steps, which is tricky in glass slippers. One broke when he tripped. As he stopped to pick up the pieces, the clock struck twelve.

A flurry of glitter put Bob back into his own

fuzzy skin and Cindy back into her torn, tattered frock.

Charming, without a horse beneath him, fell on his you-know-what.

"Where's my horse?" he asked. Then he looked at the servant girl. "Who are you?"

Cindy tossed her hair and flared her nostrils.

Charming looked into her eyes. "Do you like horses?" he asked.

"Love them," she said.

And the two walked off to see his stable and make wedding plans.

Alone, Bob scurried back to the library and chewed a nice roomy nest in an overstuffed throne. He's lived there ever since—reading and baking, baking and reading—except when Cindy visits her in-laws and brings along her children. After tea, Bob tells the children a story or two, and then they run outside to dress the Queen's cats in doll clothes and send them down the hill in a baby carriage.

Back at the cottage, the witch rotted into a stinky puddle of moldy mush. Because once a pumpkin, all one can turn into is that. Or a pie.

Happily Ever After

"I remember that ball," said Muffin. "The smoked salmon was divine!"

"I remember that horse," said Brutus. "She almost stepped on me."

"Wait a minute," said Muffin, looking at the rat and thinking hard. "You bake cookies—just like Bob." Her tail swished while she considered the coincidence. "And Cindy visits you all the time!" A light flashed in her eyes. "So if the horse was Cindy," she reasoned, "then the maiden must have been . . ." She studied the rat's face. "What am I saying? You couldn't be. I mean, you're too short, and besides . . ."

"Maybe you're on to something, Muffin," said Brutus. His eyes narrowed. "Was that *you* in that dress, Mack?"

"The name's Bob, sir, but yes . . . yes, it was," said Bob.

"Well, Bob," said Brutus, "you looked great."

"Thanks," said Bob. "*You* look great in doll clothes—especially that little blue bonnet."

"You really do, Brutus," said Muffin.

"Thanks," said Brutus, washing his paw.

"So, do you know any more rat stories?"

"Nope," said Bob, "that's all there is."

"Then tell us again!" begged Muffin.

"You'd listen to them all over again?" asked Bob.

"Yes!" said Muffin.

"You wouldn't eat me halfway through?"

"I guess not," said Brutus.

"Thanks!" said Bob. "You're a pal. But I'm all storied out."

"Then we might as well eat you," said Brutus.

"Might as well," said Bob. "Unless—"

"Unless what?" said Muffin.

"Unless you want me to write all the stories down. Then you could read them whenever you want."

"Oh yes!" said Muffin.

"Do it," said Brutus.

Muffin fetched pen and paper. Brutus found some ink.

"I can't do it here," said Bob.

"Why not?" said Muffin.

"I need quiet," said Bob. "I need to be alone . . . perhaps in the library."

"We're not allowed in the library," said Muffin.

"That's a shame," said Bob. "But I promise to have the stories ready by morning."

Brutus looked doubtful.

"With pictures?" asked Muffin.

"Sure," said the rat.

"Well, okay," said Brutus. "And then we'll have you for breakfast."

"Of course," said Bob.

In the morning, when Bob had written the last word of the last tale, Brutus and Muffin were still asleep on the Queen's feather bed. Bob could hear them snoring.

But they would wake up, and soon.

The rat paced back and forth, thinking and

thinking and thinking some more. If he tried
to run away, they would catch him. If he tried to
hide, they would sniff him out. There was no
escape.

He glimpsed the pink and orange sunrise
through the library window. It was spellbinding.

Spellbinding?

Bob's memory raced back to Twinkle's book
of spells. He could see it before him—big and fat,
with a spell for every possible problem. In his
mind's eye, he flipped through the pages. And
there it was!

Then, before you could say "Bob's your
uncle," Bob said this:

> *"Blue goose, true goose,*
> *skimming-through-the-sky goose,*
> *find me, fly me—*
> *Save me from the stew, goose!"*

And before you could say "Justine's your aunt," Blue Sue flapped up to the window and honked.

Bob hopped on Sue's back, and together they flew to another library in another kingdom— where Bob read to his heart's content and they both lived happily ever after.

ABOUT THE AUTHOR

MARY HANSON is the author of several books for children, including *The Difference Between Babies & Cookies* and *The Old Man and the Flea*. A retired children's librarian, Mary enjoys reading (sometimes to her cats), coaching high school mock trials (always with her husband), and looking forward to visits from her two children, who grew up against her wishes and went away to college. Her favorite cookies are chocolate-layered toffee crackers.

ABOUT THE ILLUSTRATOR

JOHN HENDRIX's illustrations have appeared in the *New Yorker*, the *New York Times*, and *Rolling Stone*, among others. He is the illustrator of one book for children, also involving rats: *The Giant Rat of Sumatra: or Pirates Galore*, by Sid Fleischman. John currently lives in Saint Louis with his wife, Andrea, and their son, Jack, and teaches illustration at Washington University. He loves shortbread cookies with icing and sprinkles.